The Ghoul of Bodger O'Toole

*Look out for more Ghostly Tales
from Penny Dolan...*

The Spectre of Hairy Hector
The Ghost of Able Mabel
The Phantom of Billy Bantam

The Ghoul of Bodger O'Toole

Penny Dolan

illustrated by Philip Hopman

■SCHOLASTIC

To Laurian, Ed, Finn, Breandan and Conn,
with much love.

Scholastic Children's Books,
Commonwealth House, 1-19 New Oxford Street,
London, WC1A 1NU, UK
a division of Scholastic Ltd
London ~ New York ~ Toronto ~ Sydney ~ Auckland
Mexico City ~ New Delhi ~ Hong Kong

First published by Scholastic Ltd, 2004

ISBN 0 439 96874 7

Printed and bound by Nørhaven Paperback A/S, Denmark

2 4 6 8 10 9 7 5 3 1

Chapter One

High on the coach roof sat Davey, among the bags and bundles. Wind and weather blasted him, and the rope hobbling his ankles was tied so tightly that he couldn't leap free. Sometimes he woke, and sometimes he slept, but the horses raced on and on.

Nobody back at the workhouse had told Davey where he was going, or whom he was going to. "You've been sent for," was all they'd said. "May be good. May be bad. Who knows?"

At last the coach clattered to a stop by the signpost at Trewary Cross. Davey lifted his weary head, and was surprised by sunlight and yellow gorse and purple heather.

"One delivery. Workhouse boy, as promised!" yelled the coach driver.

He shoved so hard that Davey tumbled down like a parcel. He fell at the hooves of a handsome stallion carrying a tall rider. The man's coat was elegant, but behind his long moustache, his smile seemed as thin as a blade.

"Looks like your master's here, workhouse boy, so watch your manners!" scoffed the driver.

"Not this time," the rider drawled. "Grown lads like him need too much feeding. I'm after a starveling that's bolted. Run off. Gone." He twitched his horsewhip. "Seen anyone, have you?"

"No, not a soul," the driver promised, cringing.

"Then be on your way, dolt," the dark rider snapped.

"Yes, sir! Certainly, sir! But if I should catch your runaway, where should I send him?"

"Ha! To me, Young Mallion, care of Old Man Mallion's Mansion, of course!"

The horseman pointed across to a far headland. There, high above everything, was a large grey house with cold, glittering windows.

"I see, sir. Thank ye, Master Mallion, sir."
The driver shook his reins, and hurried
the coach away.

As Davey struggled up
from the dust, the horseman
circled around him.

"Maybe a lad like you would be useful...?"
Mallion taunted.

Davey glanced around despairingly. Who
was coming for him? He couldn't bear the
thought of working for this man. His clothes
might be rich and fine, but his eyes were as
cold and hard as granite rock. There'd be no
scrap of kindness in such a master.

Just then a tall stranger came bounding across the heather, shouting a friendly welcome. "Halloooooo, Davey! Halloooooo!" At the sight of Davey's hobbled legs, he drew out his pocket knife, and sliced the rope away in disgust. "That better?" he said.

"Who are you?" asked Davey, anxiously.

"Don't you recognize me, lad?" the stranger smiled. "Have you forgotten?"

Davey paused, and blinked. Yes, there was something familiar about that smiling face. A memory stirred in the back of Davey's mind. Could it be? After seven long years? He barely had the courage to ask.

"Are you… Are you my big brother? Are you Trevick?"

The young man chuckled, and ruffled Davey's hair. "Who else could I be but Trevick?" He stared boldly up at the rider. "This lad is my own young brother," he stated, "and he's come here to live with me, not as one of your slaveys, Mallion!"

Young Mallion gave an evil laugh. "If this weevil is sharing your home by the shore, remember to tell him the place is haunted." He spurred his horse to a gallop, and sped off across the moor.

"Haunted? You're wrong, Mallion!" Trevick yelled after him. "That's just a stupid old tale."

Haunted? Davey thought, alarmed. He had no time to find out. Trevick was already asking about his journey. "So that workhouse warden didn't say I'd sent for you?" Trevick groaned. "Oh no! Didn't I promise I'd get you back, Davey?"

"Yes, Trevick, you did," Davey mumbled, thinking of the day the orphan brothers were parted. The tiny Davey had been sent to struggle for crusts at the workhouse. The young Trevick had been sent to sail on dangerous oceans. Davey had hardly dared hope he'd see his brother again. So now he felt too dazed to speak.

"This can be our new beginning," Trevick beamed, slapping Davey cheerfully on the back. "Let's start with the supper that's waiting for you, little brother. Come on!"

Off went Trevick along the sheep-paths that ran through the heather. Davey followed, slowly at first, then faster. Soon he was running free in the bright, clear air.

It was amazing to feel alive again.

As the ground began to slope, Trevick stopped and held out a warning arm. "Not so fast, lad, or you'll fly right over the cliff."

"Oh!" gasped Davey, crashing thankfully into Trevick.

From the edge, he saw how the path twisted steeply down to a small harbour. The bay glittered like blue glass. Only the sharp rocks further out at sea hinted at storms and shipwrecks.

"That's Trewary Cove, and those are the Doom Rocks, and see that?" Trevick smiled, pointing to a small cottage along the curve of the nearest headland. "That's Bodger's Yard! Our new home, Davey-boy."

Davey pinched himself, but nothing disappeared. He looked up at his long-lost brother, and began to laugh aloud. "Thank you, Trevick," he cried. "Thank you!" It was wonderful.

As Davey was halfway down the cliff path, a gull flew at him, screeching. Suddenly Mallion's words came back into Davey's mind. Bodger's Yard was his new home – and Bodger's Yard was haunted? It couldn't be, it couldn't. He'd ask Trevick about it as soon as he had the chance.

Chapter Two

Soon Trevick and Davey were crunching
along the shingle.

Bodger's Yard was a wide grassy ledge,
well above the shore. The small cottage
stood at one end. A slipway of well-worn
rocks slid gently to the sea at the front, while
the tall cliff rose steeply up at the back.

As they drew closer, Davey saw the stone walls surrounding Bodger's Yard had crumbled. The cottage door was peeling, and roof slates were missing here and there. The uneven yard was littered with seaweed and old fish-bones. Even the cliff face behind was covered with bushes and overgrown brambles. It seemed half-deserted.

"I've had no time to tidy up outside," Trevick apologized.

"That's all right," Davey smiled, "I can help you with it, now I'm here."

The scent of supper wafted round them as they stepped through the door. Inside, the cottage was as ship-shape as an admiral would want. Trevick had worked really hard. Davey gazed round the welcoming room, and had to blink away the itch of tears.

True, there were several pots and pans about, in case rain leaked through the roof. Apart from that, the place was cosy indeed. There were shelves full of boxes and bottles, cans and canisters, and rare shells and souvenirs from Trevick's travels. Davey went to the jug and basin in the corner, and soaped away the grime of his journey. He hesitated, not sure what to do next, but Trevick pulled out one of the chairs.

"Sit down at the table, do. I'm starved to shreds already." Trevick chuckled, cracking four eggs into the frying pan.

"You were no taller than a table leg last time we ate together, Davey," he added.

Davey nodded sadly. Soon they were munching on bacon and eggs and buttery potatoes, and Davey ate as he had not eaten in ages.

As he took his last mouthful, his head flopped forward.

Trevick smiled. "Time for bed." He'd made a neat, hide-away bunk for Davey, high among the rafters, with a rope ladder and its own sailcloth curtain. "You'll be as snug as a bug in a rug up there," he said.

Trevick's room, a narrow space crammed with maps and charts, lay at the back of the cottage.

Davey clambered into his bunk, remembering the hard beds and stale sheets at the workhouse. Ugh! He slid thankfully under the clean covers, and listened as Trevick cleared the table, and went off to read in his own room.

For a moment Davey sat up, and peeped through the tiny window by his bed. Trevick's lantern sent a shimmer across the waves of Trewary Cove. The thought of the ghastly ghost popped into Davey's head.

"It can just pop out again. I'm too tired to care," Davey murmured sleepily, pulling the blankets up around his shoulders. He closed

his eyes, and, for the first time in many
years, felt happy.

"Goodnight, Trevick!" he called.
"Goodnight, Davey!"
"Goodnight."
"Goodnight!"

Over the next few weeks, Davey and Trevick
worked and joked and chatted, and got to
know each other again. They had the yard
to clear, the paving slabs to set firm,
and the leaking roof to fix too.

Davey eyed the tangle of brambles and
briars clambering up the cliff face. They
almost looked as if they were hiding
something. "When do we start on those?"
he asked.

"Not for a while," Trevick answered. "We've
got plenty to do here."

Bit by bit, Davey settled into his new life. He enjoyed helping Trevick, and he loved wandering freely by the shore, skimming pebbles far, far out to sea. Davey felt free and happy, and he put the tale of the boat-yard ghost right out of his head.

Then, one evening, when he was alone in the yard, he heard a strange moaning, groaning sound. Perhaps it was just the echo of big waves booming against the Doom Rocks, but perhaps not. Davey hurried indoors, just in case.

He noticed something else too. Whenever the two brothers went along to the harbour, folk chatted to Trevick, friendly-like.

But folk never, ever came to chat at the cottage. In fact, they seemed more scared by Bodger's Yard than they were by Mallion's far-off mansion.

* * *

A few days later Trevick came in grinning. He'd got a bit of work building a barn at a nearby farm, so his head was dazed with daydreams.

"Maybe there'll be wood left over," said Trevick, as they sat by the fire. "Maybe they'll give me those timbers, and maybe I can build my very own boat at last. Maybe, when that's done, we'll make another, and maybe another, and Bodger's Yard will be a proper boatyard again, and maybe—"

"Trevick!" Davey burst out. "Tell me one thing. Is Bodger's Yard haunted?"

"Haunted? No. That's just rot and rats' tails," said Trevick, a touch too quickly.

"You've got to tell me," said Davey, "if you're leaving me here by myself."

Trevick sighed sadly. "All I can tell you is what I've heard, Davey," he said, and stared at the fire for a while before beginning.

"Many years ago, a stranger came to Trewary Cove. Some say he'd been a sailor, like me. His name was Tam O'Toole. He was as big and strong as an ox, and clever with his hands. He built this cottage, and the yard, and boats.

"But every boat Tam built brought bad luck. His first boat burnt to ashes overnight. The second drifted from its moorings and smashed. The third sank in the bay, full of holes, or so it was said. Then Old Man Mallion, who ran the Mallion boatyard only three bays away—"

"Young Mallion's grandfather?" asked Davey.

"Yes, him," said Trevick. "He swore that Tam's work was botched from start to finish. He claimed Tam bodged his boats together from rotten timbers and rusty nails. Old Mallion's tales spread wide, as bad tales do, especially when rich men tell 'em. Soon folk were calling the poor, ashamed soul 'Bodger' to his face."
Trevick shook his head, disgusted.

"So what happened then?" Davey urged.

"There was some sort of contest – a race around the Doom Rocks, so they say."

"Did Tam win?" asked Davey hopefully.

Trevick shook his head. "No. He and his boat went down beyond the bay. Old Man Mallion made it back, of course. Some say Bodger's ghost is still about the yard, wanting revenge!"

Trevick chuckled, and winked at his young brother. "That silly, spooky story made this place cheap enough for me to buy, Davey. In a way, the Ghoul of Bodger O'Toole gave us this home, so I'm grateful – especially as I've seen no sign he's around."

At that moment a burning log slipped in the grate, sending a shower of sparks on to the hearth. They jumped, then burst out laughing.

"Maybe when my boat's built, Davey, it'll be the best in all Trewary Cove," Trevick declared, "and maybe folk will come hurrying to Bodger's Yard again."

"So there's nothing to worry about?" asked Davey, feeling relieved.

Trevick rubbed his chin. "Nothing – though Young Mallion might start worrying when Bodger's Yard is back in action." Trevick gave a confident grin. "Do I care? No!" he proclaimed, and waved the toasting fork about triumphantly. "Time to cut some more slices of bread, please, Davey."

* * *

As Trevick was busy at the farm, Davey started to collect water from their well along the cliff path, when they needed it. The well was a deep rocky hollow, where a fresh-water spring swirled about on its way to the salty sea. Trevick had made a wooden lid to stop sheep slipping down the hole, and to keep the water clean.

Each time, Davey slid the lid away, lowered the bucket down on a rope, and hauled it up again. He slid the lid back, and carried the bucket to the cottage without spilling a drop.

Then, one morning, the lid wasn't in place. Davey knew he'd put it back before. It happened that evening, and the next morning too. Davey replaced the lid properly each time, and he didn't tell Trevick.

"I'm in charge of the water now, aren't I?" he said to himself. "So I'll solve the problem."

Chapter Three

That evening, as he walked to the well, Davey clattered the bucket as loudly as he could. He whistled and sang as he filled it up with water, and rattled the lid about. Then he stomped off homewards, but he didn't go far. He hid behind a bush, and soon he heard someone scrabbling down the cliff.

A tiny figure darted out, dragged the lid away, and lowered something down on a string into the gurgling well. A moment later the teeny water-pincher pulled it up again. Davey darted forward, and seized the arm of a small, ragged boy.

"What are you doing at our well?" he asked firmly.

"Let me go! Let me go! Let me go!" The little lad screamed and screeched and fought. A clay bottle fell from his hand. It hit the stones with a crack, and water spilt across the grass.

At this, the small boy flung himself down and wailed. He was covered in filthy scratches and berry stains, as if he'd been living wild.

"Stay here, tiddler," Davey said softly. "Don't worry. I'll bring you something to use instead of your broken bottle. But you must put the lid back on the well, or the water might go foul."

Davey had just turned towards home when a clump of grass caught him hard between the shoulderblades. "Ouch! What on earth...?" he gasped.

"Go away, you and your ghosty bogle!" the little boy howled, scrambling away up the cliff. "Don't want any ghoulie ghosties coming after me!"

Davey ran after him, but the raggy lad had gone. Nevertheless, when Davey got back home he found a tin mug with a strong handle and tied on some new string, so the boy could get water from the well. He cut a thick slice of crusty bread and layered it with jam. Then he took them all down to the well, and left them there.

When he crept back ten minutes later, his gifts had disappeared, and the lid was carefully in place.

* * *

That night Davey lay wide awake, thinking of the ragged lad and his talk of the ghostly bogle. Davey had told Trevick about the mysterious groaning and moaning he kept hearing, but Trevick insisted it was the sea.

If that ghoul's still about, Davey worried, maybe he'll bodge things up for us, and botch all Trevick's plans.

It was long after midnight when he fell asleep, with the wild sea booming through his dreams.

Davey woke to bright daylight. He pulled on his clothes, and padded, muddle-headed, to the open door. The blue sea rippled in the bay, and birds swooped around the cottage roof. Trevick was at home today, singing away in the yard. Davey grinned, and put his midnight frights away. He'd give Trevick a hand sorting out some new roof slates. Then, later, he might start exploring those brambly briars.

Chapter Four

As soon as the last slates were slipped into place, Trevick took his best jacket and buckled boots out of his old sea chest.

"There's a cart going over to Pennyworth Market," he said. "I need a few things. Do you want to come?"

Davey wanted to go, but he wanted to explore the hidden cliff-face even more. "No, thank you," he said.

"Don't do anything daft while I'm gone, will you?" Trevick said.

"Nothing daft," Davey answered, waving Trevick on his way. If he hurried to the well, he'd have time to search that cliff before evening came on.

Davey picked up a spare pasty for the ragged boy and headed for the well, but there was no sign of the child. He quickly filled his bucket, ready to collect later, then wandered further round the headland, and out on to the big rocks that guarded the bay.

There was no shelter here. The wind pushed and pulled him about, and the waves crashed between gigantic boulders. Above the swish of the sea and the roar of the surf, he heard the screech of seabirds.

Davey listened again, horrified. Those weren't gulls' cries. Someone was calling for help! He scrambled over rocks, peering down into crevices full of foaming water, searching and searching.

The ragged boy was caught in a deep
gully, trapped by the incoming tide. He clung
to a rocky ledge, with seaweed swirling
round his tiny shoulders. Davey flung himself
down on the rocks, and grasped the scruff
of the child's neck
as firmly as
he could.

Bit by bit, he hauled the child up out of the sea, and dragged him to a smooth, safe boulder. The boy was blue with cold. Salt water streamed from his hair and nose.

"My fish…" wailed the child hungrily, staring at a thin line floating out to sea. One skinny fish drifted on the bent pin. He'd been trying to find food.

Davey took the pasty from his pocket. "Eat this instead?" he asked. The crust was broken, but it smelt good. The boy seized the pasty, and nibbled away.

"Listen, tiddler," Davey said. "You can't live out on the cliffs any more. Come with me and see my big brother Trevick." The boy squinted up, quivering with dread. Davey tried to act strong. "Don't be afraid. The yard's perfectly safe. I'll make sure Bodger won't get you."

The child grinned, and nodded. If Davey had saved him from the sea, surely he could see off any old ghosties? He thrust a grubby fist in Davey's hand, and shook it.

"Good," said Davey, rather anxiously. "Now let's get back to the well."

* * *

Back at the cottage, Davey found Trevick's warmest jumper, and wrapped it round the child. He sat him on the doorstep.

"What's your name?" asked Davey.

"Tigg. Just Tigg," said the boy, wiping his salt-stained face. "That's all."

"Where did you come from, Tigg?" asked Davey, although he'd guessed the answer already.

"There!" Tigg scowled, pointing across the bay. He stuck his tongue out at the grey mansion on the far-off moor.

"Master Mallion was very horrible to me, so I ran away, and hid on your cliff." He gave a small, sad sigh. "But it's very hungry living there, you know."

"And dangerous too?" Davey reminded him.

"Not as dangerous as living in Bodger's haunted house, like you, Davey," Tigg said admiringly. He wriggled happily in his overgrown jumper. "You aren't one bit scared of ghosties, are you? You'll look after Tigg, won't you, Davey?"

Davey gulped. "Of course," he replied, "but now I want you to stay on this step, and watch for my big brother Trevick. I've got to do something important, all by myself. You stay right here! Understand?"

Tigg answered with a huge grin, so at last Davey set off for the cliff.

Chapter Five

Davey clambered over fallen rocks. He
struggled through narrow spaces between
the twisting twigs, among the strands of nets
and twine, and broken feathers. It was hard
to see what was ahead. Davey pushed
through gaps, this way and that, and found
himself close to the foot of the cliff. He was
facing a pair of doors, as faded and
bleached as the rock itself. They were set
into the cliff, and were so big and wide that

an ox could pass through them. Davey tugged at the rusty handle, and one door grated open. He could just squeeze through.

A shaft of afternoon sunlight stretched into the darkness, revealing an enormous cave.

"Hello?" Davey called.

His voice boomed back, sending bats scattering through the gloom. The dry floor was littered with discarded odds and ends. Planks were stacked here and there. Hammers and saws lay in the dust. There were clusters of bolts and boxes of nails.

"Carpenter's tools!" Davy smiled. "They'll be useful to Trevick." Then he gasped. "Oh no! This must be Bodger's old store!"

Ahead, in the middle of the cave, loomed the bones of a huge skeleton. Davey trembled with fear. Was it the bones of old Bodger? But as he crept closer, he saw it was the wooden ribs of a half-built boat.

"Wow!" said a small voice, close behind him.

"Tigg?" Davey whirled round. "Who said you could come in?"

"Me!" Tigg told him. "Is this old Bodger's cave?"

"It's Trevick's cave!" said Davey, rather nervously.

Tigg wasn't worried at all. He scampered about, dodging under planks and around barrels. But the boat, and the thought of the ghoul returning, made Davey anxious.

"Come on!" he said. "We're leaving."

He tugged Tigg out of the cave, and closed the huge door again.

At once Davey felt happier. Huh! Stupid stories! Just wait till he told Trevick about those good strong timbers. Now his big brother could build his boat, and things would be perfect – once he'd explained about Tigg, of course.

Chapter Six

It wasn't long before Trevick came striding down the cliff path. Davey rushed to meet him, crowing, "Come and see what I've found!"

As soon as Trevick saw the wood in the cave, he clapped Davey's back. "Well done, Davey-boy! This is a real miracle! A dream come true!" Stroking the sturdy timber frame, he smiled. "We'll have this boat on the sea in no time."

"Trevick, I've got something else to show you," Davey added quietly. "It's in the cottage."

"What sort of else?" asked Trevick, chuckling as they went through the door.

"This sort of else."

Tigg stood on the hearth rug, glaring at Trevick. Davey pushed Tigg forward, but he clung close as a puppy to Davey's side.

"This is Mallion's runaway, Tigg. He was living out on the cliff," Davey explained.

Trevick scratched his head. "Well, I'm blowed," he said, and gave an enormous smile. "Well, you don't look big enough to slave for anyone, and certainly not Mister Mallion." Trevick leaned forward. "Are you hungry, Tigg?" he whispered.

Tigg looked puzzled. "Hungry?" Then, beaming back at Trevick, Tigg stepped forward. He fished the tin mug from his pocket, set it on the table, and pulled up a nearby stool. "Hungry!" he said, proudly.

Trevick got out one more bowl. "How about some soup, eh?" He reached for the ladle, and lifted the lid off the cooking pot. "Sit down, little 'un, and you too, Davey," he said. "There'll be enough for three."

They had a good meal, finishing with the plum cake Trevick had brought back from the market. Then Davey sat by the fire with Tigg, and showed him how to play five stones with tiny pebbles from the beach. "Throw up one, and catch up two. Throw up one, and catch up three…" Davey explained. Soon Tigg could snatch up stones quite swiftly.

Trevick dragged in an empty log box, lined it with an old quilt, and set it against the wall. "This box-bed will just fit a mite like you, Tigg, if you curl up," he said. "Davey's bunk is just up there, so you needn't feel scared."

* * *

That night, as Davey snuggled down under his covers, he called out.

"Goodnight, Trevick. Goodnight Tigg."

"Goodnight, little brother," said Trevick.

"Goodnight, big Davey," came a small voice. "Goodnight, tall Trevick!"

"Goodnight!"

"Goodnight again!" the small voice giggled.

"Goodnight, Tigg! Go to sleep!"

"Goodnight, Davey and Trevick!"

"GOODNIGHT EVERYONE!" called Trevick, very firmly. "NOW!"

As Davey drifted off to sleep, he felt contented. Tigg was safe, and Trevick had plans for the half-made boat. Hmmm! If the ghostly Bodger was around, would he be contented too?

* * *

The next day Trevick and Davey were up at dawn, hacking down the brambles and briars, and shifting the boulders that blocked the entrance. Once everything was cleared away, they opened the doors wide. A straight path led from the store to the slipway and the sea.

Then they started on the cave. Trevick began by putting lanterns here and there, so they could have light if they needed it. Davey and Trevick tidied all the old tools away, and Tigg helped pick up spilt nails and tipped-over tacks. Someone had left here in a hurry, and never returned. Gradually, they got Bodger's cave back into working order. The skeleton timbers stood waiting in the centre of all.

"Tomorrow we'll begin on our boat!" Trevick said, dancing with joy.

* * *

The next morning they started on the task. The boat needed a lot more work, even with such a finely made frame. Luckily, they discovered a stack of curving planks hidden under a weatherworn sail. "Just right to shape the hull," beamed Trevick.

Trevick stood outside the boat, hammering his planks on to the timber ribs. *Bang, bang, bang!* Young Davey worked inside the hull, forcing a wooden block hard against the curving planks, so Trevick's nails would bite into them firmly. Layer by layer, day by day, the skeleton turned into a true boat.

Sometimes Tigg played, sometimes he helped, but often he strutted around the yard with a pocket full of pebbles. He always seemed to have them with him.

"Why have you got those, nipper?" asked Trevick. "Do you want to skim stones like Davey?"

Tigg shook his head. "In case the old ghoulie-man appears," he said with a scowl, rattling them.

"Not that sea-dog's tale again?" snickered Trevick. "Well, if there was a Ghoul of Bodger O'Toole, I'd like to thank him for this boat, and the great times we'll be having soon!"

Davey laughed, but deep down he wished that Trevick wouldn't joke so. How would the phantom feel about someone else finishing the boat he'd begun? Davey was sure that the ghost was about. Sometimes he sensed something watching from the shadows. Often the lantern candles snuffed out without warning. Trevick said it was air gusting through the cave, but he was less sure.

* * *

At last they stood in the cave with aching arms, admiring the finished hull. She was only a small boat for getting around the coves and the coast, but as the sun streamed through the open doors, her sides shone like smooth satin. She was beautiful!

Trevick was tired, but happy. "Tomorrow we'll move her out into the yard."

Davey felt Tigg tugging at his sleeve. "Done now? Hungry now?" pleaded the small boy, ever hopeful.

"Yes, Tigg," chuckled Trevick. "We're done. We're hungry. Lunchtime?"

They sat on the stone wall, munching slabs of bread and cheese happily. Tigg ran about, tossing spare crumbs to the gulls.

Suddenly Davey spotted a man galloping across the shore towards them. The rider's hair was as dark as his horse's mane. He wore a silk scarf around his throat, and a pistol tucked in his leather belt.

Spray leapt from the pounding hooves.

"Young Mallion!" exclaimed Trevick, choking on his lunch.

Little Tigg gave a cry of terror, and dashed into the cottage.

By the time the rider had reached them, Trevick was ready. "What do you want, sir?" he asked.

Mallion's hand rested on his pistol, but his eyes fired hate. "My telescope tells me you've been busy in that old store. Building a boat are we, Mister Trevick?" he asked, attempting to peer into the cave.

"That I am," Trevick answered peacefully. "And did you enjoy spying on me from your mansion then?"

Mallion's gloved fist writhed angrily. "The only boats built around these bays are my boats, made by my men! Mallion boats!" he shouted. "Bad things happen to those who go against me. Do you understand, Mister Trevick?"

"I can build boats if I choose," Trevick replied defiantly.

"Then tell me this. Do you think your boat a good boat?" asked Mallion, his smile twisting like a serpent.

"She'll be as sweet as a sea-breeze," said Trevick simply.

"No," scoffed Mallion, "like any boat from Bodger's Yard, she'll sink as soon as she leaves the shore, I promise you."

"How can you say that?" Davey cried.

The frame he'd found was neither botched nor bodged. Whoever had carved those timbers would never make boats that sank or split. As Davey heard Mallion's threatening words, he felt sure he knew where the damage had come from. Somehow, Old Man Mallion had secretly destroyed Bodger's boats and, in the end, poor Bodger too. Davey grew anxious. This time it was Young Mallion brimming over with malice. Trevick should be wary.

"Any boat of mine will be swift and sure, Mister Mallion," Trevick replied quietly.

"She won't," Mallion's face had a sharp, fox-like look.

"She will."

"She won't!"
Mallion sneered.

"She will,"
snapped Trevick.
"She will, every
inch of her!"

"Ha!" Mallion gave a cunning grin. "Well then, Mister Trevick, prove it! Race her against one of my boats. Just a small race: out to the Doom Rocks and back – say, tomorrow evening?"

"Fair and true?" Trevick asked. "Like against like?"

Mallion nodded. "But a bet would add interest," he said. "So how about this, Mister Trevick? Win, and you build boats at Bodger's Yard without trouble from me. Lose, and you leave Bodger's Yard for good." He paused, then added, "And you hand over the little lad who's hiding at your place. Thank you so much for feeding him up for me!"

"Tigg?" cried Davey, his heart sinking.

"Yes, the wretched Tigg! I'd spied him out days ago."

"And when we win?" asked Trevick, swift and fearless.

"Pardon?"

"When we win, what about Tigg?" insisted Trevick.

"Oh, you can keep the useless child!" sniffed Mallion.

"Do you truly promise?" demanded Trevick. "Especially about Tigg?"

"Of course."

"Then, Mister Mallion," said Trevick "I accept your challenge!"

Mallion threw his head back and laughed aloud. "Then you're a born fool, Mister Trevick, like Bodger before you," he cried, cantering back across the sand.

Davey gaped at his big brother. "You agreed?"

"What else could I do, Davey? She's a sound, strong boat – and how else can we save Tigg?" Trevick gazed out at the distant Doom Rocks, and went pale. It would be a tough race, for sure.

Tigg crept out of the cottage, the pebbles rattling as ever in his pockets. He sidled up to Trevick. "You will win, won't you?" he whispered anxiously. Trevick smiled bravely, but could not answer.

"Of course we will," said Davey, quickly. "Don't you worry, Tigg. We'll win."

Chapter Seven

Just after midnight Davey woke, and the hair bristled on his neck. He could hear that moaning, groaning sound, coming from across the yard. He slipped from his bunk, ran outside, and edged through the door of the store. A shimmering half-human shape was hunched over Trevick's precious boat.

The huge creature wore old sailor's garments, and its hair was twisted into a thin pigtail. A wide belt studded with tools and hammers and bulging bags of nails hung round its waist. Its two tattooed arms lovingly stroked the gleaming boat while it groaned in misery.

It's him! It's the Ghoul of Bodger O'Toole! thought Davey aghast.

Just then, the ghoul gave an awful, despairing cry. It lifted one hammer and smashed a mighty blow at the wooden boat. The hull split and splintered, and a great hole appeared.

"Hey!" Davey shouted, without hesitation. "You stop that, Bodger O'Toole!"

Too late! Davey drew in a sudden breath as the thing turned towards him. Two round, bloodshot eyes fixed on him. This thing had been human once, but now it was a ghostly, ghastly ghoul, glowing with unearthly light. An awful toothless grin stretched across its broad cheeks. The ghoul growled menacingly, and lurched towards Davey.

"Who stole my boat?" it roared in a voice as rough as sandpaper. "Who stole my boat?"

Davey backed away. What could he say?
They'd known the timber frame must have
been Bodger's work. "We weren't meaning to
steal your boat!" he said.

The ghoul's eyes widened ominously. "But
you did," it moaned. "You found Bodger's
secret boat, and you stole it!"

"Trevick and I were just finishing it off."
Davey stammered, darting behind a stack of
wood.

"To steal it away!" The ghoul plodded closer.

"No! Yes! Maybe!" cried Davey. "We didn't
know you still wanted it, and Mallion—"

The ghoul's huge
hand darted forward,
and froze around Davey's
throat. "Mallion? You are
one of Mallion's men?" A look
of utter misery passed over its bloated
features. It gave a shuddering groan. "Will
I never have peace?"

"Of course we're not Mallion's men,"
Davey croaked breathlessly. "He's trying to
get rid of us too. We've got to race our boat
– your boat – against Mallion tomorrow
night, or he'll seize the yard—"

A tiny voice pierced the air. "And that
Mallion's a very, very horrid man," shrilled
Tigg, pattering into the cave.

The monstrous creature slowly turned and stared at the small child, dressed in a nightshirt, who was smiling up at him. Absentmindedly, the ghoul let go of Davey, who slid to the floor. Tigg's eyes were as big as saucers. He gazed admiringly at the huge figure of Bodger O'Toole. He forgot all about the stones still in his pockets.

"Wow! You really are a big scary ghoulie-man, aren't you?" he gasped. "You must be the best ghostie ever, ever in the whole wide world!" Suddenly, Tigg spotted the broken boat. "And did you make that big hole all by yourself?" he asked. "Poor boat! You must be a really, really strong ghostie!"

The ghoul's toothless mouth seemed to widen into a strange, shy smile. An idea flashed through Davey's mind. He took his chance. "Bet you couldn't mend it, though," he declared.

The ghoul roared, and thumped its mighty chest. "Bodger could mend it!"

"Bet you couldn't!" gulped Davey.

Two bloodshot eyes stared into Davey's face. He smelt the stench of rotten wood, and ancient seaweed. "Bet I could!" the ghoul grinned.

"Before morning?" Davey insisted, pushing his luck.

The ghoul raised its huge, scarred fists towards the ceiling. "Huh! Morning! Just you wait and see!" It picked up one piece of splintered plank, and another. "Poor boat! Better soon," it crooned. "Bodger make you better. There, there. We'll show that Mallion man."

Davey backed towards the cave door, grabbing little Tigg as he went. He charged out of Bodger's cave, heaved the door shut, and scrambled across the yard.

"What now?" said Tigg.

"Now we keep our fingers crossed," said Davey, "and it's back-to-bed time too!"

Chapter Eight

Davey lay in his bunk, listening to the
hammering and sawing, and the mournful
singing.

He felt bad about Bodger and his boat.
Trevick and he had claimed those timbers
without thinking. Bodger might be a ghostly,
ghastly ghoul, but the boat had been his to
begin with. A secret boat, so Bodger had
said. Maybe he'd kept it a secret to save it
from Mallion's men? Maybe he'd thought it
was one last chance to save his name? Davey

tossed and turned, wanting to make things fairer. At last, he worked out a way to do it.

* * *

Next morning Davey hurried to the cave. Phew! The boat had been mended perfectly. There were a few extra nails, and some new wood strengthening the damaged planking, but her hull seemed as smooth as before.

"Thank you," whispered Davey, relieved, though the cave was littered with wood shavings and sawdust.

"I'd swear somebody had been messing around in here," sighed Trevick, coming into the cave with Tigg. "Do you two know anything about it?"

Davey and Tigg glanced quickly at each other. They didn't want to worry Trevick with tales of Bodger's damage. He had enough to worry about today.

"We were playing," they fibbed.

"Well, clean it up later," was all Trevick said. "Let's get this boat outside, and ready for the race!"

They lay long logs right into the yard, like ladder rungs, then heaved the prow across the first log. "Go!" Trevick shouted, and they all pushed. The keel bumped slowly over one log and another, and the gleaming boat slid out into the daylight.

There was still a lot to do. Trevick settled her safely on wooden blocks. They fixed the rudder in place, and raised the mast. As Trevick rigged up the sails, folk came up from the harbour to watch at Bodger's Yard. "Goodness me! It's like the old days!" they said. "She's a real beauty."

"That's it," Davey decided happily. "That's the word I want."

"Time for some lunch," said Trevick. "We won't feel like eating tonight. Come on, Tigg."

"I've got something to do," Davey told
them. "I'll be in soon."

Davey searched the cave until he found
what he wanted. When he came out, he saw
that even more people had come to watch.
Davey opened the tin of bright blue paint,
took hold of a thin brush, and stood by a
smooth panel on the boat's side. He already
knew what he must write – *Bodger's Beauty*.
It felt the right name for this well-made boat.
The letters flowed on smoothly.

"That's an unlucky name to paint on your boat," called a man at the back of the crowd.

"No, it's not," Davey yelled back. "It was Bodger who began her, and she is a beautiful boat. If Mallion's men don't drill holes in her sides, or set her on fire, or do the damage they did before, she'll be better than any other craft round here." The mutters from the crowd showed many of them agreed.

Hearing the row, Trevick came out of the cottage to see what was going on. He looked at the name Davey had painted. "Well done, lad!" he said, sounding pleased. "But come and eat now, Davey. We need to get our strength up."

Davey knew Trevick was right. The sun was already lower, and in a few hours, evening would be spreading across the bay. Why had Mallion chosen such an odd time to race? Was he planning another Mallion trick? Davey had a sudden feeling they'd be needing help.

Chapter Nine

It was a calm evening, without much wind.
The sky was streaked with pale purple clouds.
Bodger's Beauty had been launched down
the slipway, and now she rocked gently in the
golden waters of the bay. All the folk in
Trewary Cove, and beyond, had arrived to
see how she did in the race. Trevick, Davey
and Tigg stood on the shore, waiting.

Around the headland came a boat, far bigger than the *Beauty*. A large lantern hung from her prow. Her sails were furled, but she moved swiftly. It was Mallion's boat, *The Magpie*. A team of expert rowers sped her along.

Trevick cursed. This wasn't like for like. If it was calm, Mallion could row more quickly. If there was wind, he could sail more swiftly. If it wasn't for Tigg standing there so eagerly, Trevick would have given in and walked away.

"Time to board the
Beauty," he said,
letting Tigg climb on
to his back. Tigg
whooped with joy
as they waded
through the shallows.

Trevick gently lifted Tigg into the boat, then
clambered in too. Hope was draining from
his heart. He looked around for Davey, but
the boy was missing. As Trevick checked the
ropes, ready for the race, his eyes were
searching the shore for his young brother.
Where could he be? What was he up to?

* * *

Davey was trembling in the darkness of the
cave. He was frightened, but he had no
other choice. If special help was needed,
there was only one person who could give it.

Davey took a deep breath, and shouted as
loud as he could. "Bodger O'Toole!" His
words mingled with the faint cheers from the

shore. "Bodger O'Toole, we need your help."
There was no answer, so he had another go.
"Come out, you Ghoul of Bodger O'Toole, or
Mallion's men will win again!"

This time the air grew icy. The ghoul
appeared. "You asked for aid from Bodger
O'Toole?" it whispered angrily. "You fool,
you fool, you stupid fool!"

Davey was angry too. He could hear
Mallion's oars splashing the waves as they
positioned *The Magpie* for the start of the
race. He'd seen how strong that boat looked.

"Listen to me, Tam O'Toole!" Davey shouted. "If ever you wanted your good name back, now is your chance. I don't care about the stupid yard, or the stupid boat, but if that Mallion wins this race, Tigg will end up as his slavey again."

"Tigg? Mallion's slavey?" The ghoul's voice was hollow as a tomb.

Davey scowled angrily. "Yes!"

The thing gave a long, low groan. "Then I will come," it said, and followed Davey out of the cave into the growing dusk.

* * *

Mallion, dressed in elegant garments, was parading up and down his boat, jeering at the smaller boat. Trevick sat in the *Beauty*, with little Tigg ready to drag up the anchor. He was looking around desperately.

"Davey!" called Trevick, then gasped as he saw the ghost. It was gliding towards the boat that, many years before, it had begun.

All along the harbour, folk froze as the glimmering ghoul floated behind Davey. "It's the Ghoul of Bodger O'Toole!" they whispered.

Mallion's face turned as white as bleached linen. He stared, spellbound, at the awful apparition, then burst into protest. "That thing cannot enter the race!"

Trevick took no notice of such cries. He looked hard at the awful, ugly creature, and saw the burning desperation in its ghastly, toothless face. "Tam O'Toole? Tam?" he called, in his kindly, friendly voice.

A look like hope lit that awful face. The bleary eyes stared at Trevick. "I was Tam, once," came the rough voice, "though that is not what they called me."

"But Tam O'Toole you are too, and it is time for you to board this boat of yours," said Trevick, moving aside to make space for the ghoul.

"Look!" cried Davey. "Can you see her name?"

The ghoul stared at the blue letters on the side of the boat.
"*Bodger's Beauty*?
My boat?" he
whispered, and
a green glow of
delight shimmered
around him.

Tigg sat open-mouthed with excitement as
Davey and then his own ghostie-man boarded
the *Beauty*. Mallion was rushing up and down
The Magpie, howling orders at his crew.

"Ready?" called Trevick. Davey nodded,
and gripped the rope. Tigg clung tight to the
side, staring up at the glowing ghoul.

The eventide bell rang out through the
growing dusk. Now, whatever happened,
boy and lad and man and ghoul, they would
be racing towards the Doom Rocks together.

Chapter Ten

Trevick and Davey were in luck at first. The little *Beauty* slipped into a swift current that drew her along. Mallion's men, stunned by the glowing ghoul, were slow to row, but gradually they moved steadily after the *Beauty*. Soon they were some distance from the harbour, and leaving the shelter of the bay. A sea-wind sprang up, and both boats hurriedly set their sails.

With her powerful sails, *The Magpie* was soon closing on the smaller boat. Davey shivered, for now he saw that lantern shine on Mallion's scheming face, laying a path of light ahead of *The Magpie*'s stern.

Through the dusk, the Doom Rocks were growing closer, like dark teeth waiting to rip any craft apart. *The Magpie* was bearing down, edging the *Beauty* towards the jagged rocks, but somehow she kept ahead.

Mallion's men had moved something on deck. "Look out!" cried Tigg, seeing the glint of metal. "A cannon!"

The ghoul groaned. "Another Mallion trick!" he cursed.

There was a flash of fire. A cannonball rained fragments into the water around them.

Trevick cried out and clutched at his arm.
As Davey grabbed the rudder,
Trevick bound the
wound tightly
with a strip of
shirt sleeve.
It was bleeding,
but not too badly.

"Good lad!" said Trevick, taking hold again. Through the dusk came the sound of the men reloading the cannon.

"Enough!" Suddenly, with a thunderous roar of fury, the ghoul flowed forward, rising like a furious figurehead at the prow of the *Beauty*. He turned his glittering gaze on Davey. "Tigg's five stones," the ghoul ordered. "Throw them hard and true, Davey!"

Squealing, Tigg tipped his precious pebbles into Davey's outstretched palm. Davey watched the rise and fall of *The Magpie* on the waves for a moment. Then he took aim. He threw straight and strong.

Four stones flew across the water, straight at Mallion's cannoneers. They hit like pistol shot, and the men stumbled about in pain.

"Last one! Go for the lantern, Davey!" croaked the ghoul. "Throw! Throw!"

Davey threw harder than he'd thought possible. He heard glass smash. The lantern blazed even brighter for a moment, then it guttered and went out, just as a cloud covered the rising moon.

Bodger himself grew dim. In the darkness, screams of confusion came from *The Magpie*.

"The Doom Rocks!" someone screeched. They had missed their way.

The submerged rocks tore into Mallion's moving boat with a dreadful roar. The villain whirled round, unable to believe what had happened. *The Magpie* rose up, then leant and tilted, and slowly the sea seemed to swallow her completely.

The ghoul reappeared, glowing even brighter, lighting the way for the *Beauty*, guiding her around the Doom Rocks and back into safer waters.

They saw the ghoul's face was grim with sorrow. "Another Mallion sent me to my death," it groaned, "and I have saved you from yours. So all is as it should be. Master Trevick, set the *Beauty* on course for home."

As they entered the cove, they heard a triumphant shouting from the harbour. Folk were waving and throwing things joyously in the air. "Welcome back, Tam O'Toole!" they shouted. "Well done, Trevick! Well done, Davey! Well done, Tigg!"

The ghoul smiled for a moment, as if anger and pain had left him. He shook little Tigg's hand, leaving a shining glow across his tiny palm. "Wow!" sighed Tigg.

Then, as the *Beauty* passed through a stretch of silvery water, the great ghoul stared straight at Davey.

"Farewell," it murmured, "and thank you. Live happily in my yard, lad, and good luck go with you and yours." There was a flickering light, and the Ghoul of Bodger O'Toole had gone.

Davey sighed and sat silently, watching Trevick laugh, and Tigg waving, and the crowds roaring with delight to welcome the *Beauty* back to the harbour again.

* * *

That night, as Davey snuggled down under
his covers, he called out.

"Goodnight, Trevick. Goodnight, Tigg."

"Goodnight, little brother," said Trevick.

"Maybe there's gold buried in Bodger's
cave?" came that small giggly voice.

"Go to sleep!"

"Gold for you, big Davey. Gold for you,
tall Trevick! Gold for me?"

"Goodnight, Tigg!"

"Goodnight again!" the small voice
laughed.

"Goodnight, Tigg! Go to sleep! NOW!"

"Goodnight, Davey and Trevick!"

"GOODNIGHT, EVERYONE!" called
Trevick, very firmly.

Davey drifted towards sleep, thinking of all that had happened. How Trevick had his boat, how he and Tigg had a welcoming home, and how the poor Ghoul of Bodger O'Toole had escaped from the lies and shame tied to his name.

"I hope you're happy, Tam O'Toole," Davey whispered, "wherever you are! Goodnight! Goodnight!"

Look out for the next book
in this shivery series!

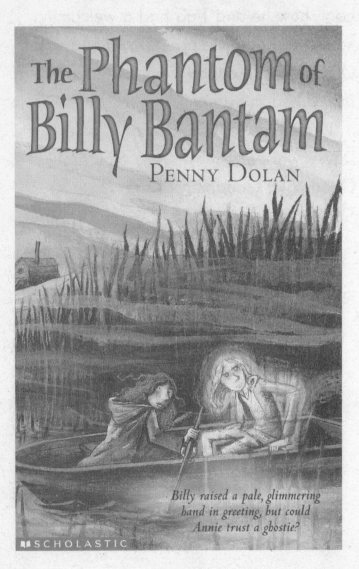

The Phantom of Billy Bantam

PENNY DOLAN

*Billy raised a pale, glimmering
hand in greeting, but could
Annie trust a ghostie?*